Hopelessly Persistent

AUTUMN JACKSON

www.weareaps.com

Table of Contents

Ever since I've known her, she's always liked me, and no matter how many times or ways I rejected her, she always came back.

All the guys in school think I'm weird or harsh. "Why keep rejecting a girl who only has eyes for you?" they ask. She's never even asked another guy out, but my response to them is simply, "I just don't like her."

How could I like her when I know nothing about her? Why would I like her when I find her absolutely annoying? She's like a fly that just won't die. Even though that persistency drives me crazy, it's her most admirable quality because I know she'll always be there.

● ● ● ● ●

I'm a girl who chooses to live a very optimistic life. My older brother and I have been through a lot even at an early age. I never let that get to me because I know we have each other. My life at school isn't too much easier; they laugh at me, and even all my friends talk about me. It's okay though because I know it'll get better. There is one honest friend I have and that's Ryan. He may seem harsh, but I know he cares. He's the only one who's ever been completely honest with me, and that includes my brother...

This is my story about how my persistency led me to my fate.

For a long time, neither me nor my brother had a stable home, and what we witnessed made him believe that we couldn't depend on anyone. That was him though, I on the other hand, never believed that people were harsh or wouldn't help, even if it appeared to be true. Nonetheless, my brother kept us away from people, and we only depended on each other. That was until we moved with Tia.

Tia was a family member we never knew we had. She was very stern and strict with us, and demanded we work at an early age. That wasn't a problem since my brother didn't feel like we could depend on her anyway. Now, here it is eight years later since we've moved in with her, and he still doesn't trust her. I like giving people the benefit of the doubt, believing everything will be okay.

CHAPTER 1

Meet Hope Stern

I was on my way to school, ready for my daily routine believing this time would be different. I know Ryan hates my persistence, but I just can't give up because I know one day, he'll like me. As I enter my first class, I see Ryan and immediately go to greet him.

"Good morning Ryan", I said cheerfully.

Ryan looked annoyed but said, "Morning".

Autumn Jackson

"How are you?" I responded.

"Same old, same old", he replied.

That's when I saw the look of anticipation and annoyance in his eyes. Despite the look he gave me, I was still cheerful. Then I said, "I have a question for you". However, he didn't

respond. So, I just asked him anyway.

"Will you go out with me?"

"No."

That was all he said. It was hard and sturdy; there was no changing his mind. Yet I still had to try.

"Please" I asked again, "Please go out with me."

"NO", he said a little harsher this time.

"But why? I asked and you aren't dating anyone, and it isn't like there's someone who wants to date you".

Ryan looked at me with an evil look in his eyes, and

said rather loudly, "I said NO", then walked away agitated.

By this time everyone had seen it, and everyone was looking at me. I didn't care; I wasn't going stop smiling. I'd try again tomorrow, and nothing would stop me. I just had to keep believing that eventually he'd give me a chance.

Not too long after Ryan's explosion, class started and everyone was talking about me, even my friends, although I never let it bother me. I wouldn't stop being me, not now or ever and I wouldn't let these people's words get to me. So, I just smiled. I smile because smiling means hope, and you can't give up. Sure, it hurt sometimes, and it's hard but the best things in life you typically must work hard for.

After class was over, my three friends came to talk to me.

"We heard about your rejection" they said, "It must've been humiliating".

"Yeah", I said with a pained smiled, "But it could've been worse".

"Worse" they exclaimed loudly, "How could it possibly be worse?"

"Well" I said after a while, "He could've gone out with me".

They all looked confused, then asked how that could be worse?

"He would've been forcing himself" I said quickly. "I don't want that".

"Girl, you do too much. This guy rejected you how many times, and now you're giving him requirements so he can date you? You must really think you all that" they added. "Either that, or you like being rejected".

"You're wrong. I don't feel that way at all about myself, nor do I like getting rejected. I just want him to like me for me, not date me out of pity. He hasn't done that, which just means I must work harder towards my goal."

"How many times have you been rejected?" they asked.

"Two thousand five hundred and forty-three" I replied quietly.

"What? And you're still going after him? You're crazy. You should just give up" they stated.

"I won't. I have faith that he will one day like me".

"Well, be prepared to get crushed because that's *ALL* that's going to happen." They said.

After that, I walked off, and was on my way home.

CHAPTER 2

Meet Cameron Stern

Once I got back home, I wasn't lonely because I had my brother, and we typically spent time together. My brother is three years older, and very protective of me. Even though he's finished with school now, he stays current with everything through me and my emotions. He can always tell when something wrong with me.

"So", he began, "How'd it go with the idiot today?"

He was referring to Ryan, and I already knew he knew the answer. My brother just wanted to see how hurt I was by it.

"He rejected me", I said with a pained smile, "Again".

My brother knew all about Ryan's rejections, and he wanted to hurt him, but never did because of me. I asked him not to.

"I don't know what you see in that idiot", my brother said for the millionth time, "But since you like him, I'll at least try to tolerate him". He then added, "That doesn't mean I won't hurt him."

I opened my mouth to protest, but my brother said he wouldn't hurt him badly. I closed my mouth because I knew this was as much of a compromise as I could expect.

Before I knew it, Tia was coming in the house. We immediately greeted her with a smile.

"Buenas tardes, Tia," I greeted.

She looked up annoyed and aggravated. I could tell today was one of those days she wasn't in the mood. She nearly knocked me down and asked how long I'd been home. Then, she turned and looked at my brother with more anger and said why he wasn't at work? I knew my Tia would be mad at my response, but I told her anyway, how I did my confession and lost track of time.

My Tia's face turned furious, and as she walked closer to me, she said, "You ungrateful brat".

And as she walked closer to me, my brother grabbed her

wrist.

He was angry and said, "Don't touch my sister."

He was very conscious of his actions, being careful not to hurt Tia. After my brother said that he took a step back, and so did Tia. After a moment, she realized what happened, walked up to my brother and smacked him. Tia told him that she would not be taking care of us forever! My brother was furious by the remark and started arguing with her. It went on for about fifteen minutes, and all I could do was think about was how all this started. It was because of my persistency; it was one of my favorite qualities, but at times like this it proved to be my worse. Despite that I'd never give it up, it's what makes me who I am.

Once my brother and Tia finally stopped arguing, he walked out to clear his mind. Not too much longer after that he came and found me in my room.

"Want to talk?" he asked.

When I didn't respond, my brother asked, "Como te sientes?"

He asked me in Spanish because he knew when I got like this, I preferred bilingual communication.

"Yo siento triste y confuse. Me siento soy complicada".

"Por que?" he asked.

"Porque I like me, but I don't like what I'm always doing" I replied.

"Well, change it" said my brother.

"Como?" I asked.

My brother responded, "Only you know. Only you know what you don't like about you, and how you should fix it".

"Pero... what if I 'fix it' and change me in the process?" I ask concerned.

"You're always changing. Just because different parts of you change doesn't mean your whole personality and inner self has changed." He informed me.

He then got up and said, "Me voy a trabajar, so if

you need anything call. Love you. And after that, he was gone, my strong big brother.

Thinking of what my brother said to me made me think.

Change but not completely. Change is only something you can do. This was a change I wanted to make; I wasn't getting rid

of my persistency, just restricting it. This way I could still be me, while reforming me.

CHAPTER 3

Let The Reformation Begin

When I got to school the next day, I decided to put my restriction to the test. I saw Ryan, but instead of asking him out like I normally do, I spoke to him and tried to have a conversation.

"Hey, Ryan."

He quickly glanced up and said, "No, I won't go out with you."

"Actually, I wasn't going to ask you out," I replied.

Ryan looked surprised and said, "What is it then?"

I was puzzled on what to say next as this was the longest I'd ever talked to Ryan without being rejected and him walking away.

"So," I asked, "how are you?"

"Fine." replied Ryan.

I thought he was going to ask me, but he never did, so I asked if he had any plans for the day.

"Nope" he said with a bored tone.

"Well, then," I said hesitantly, "Will you go out with me?"

Ryan just looked up, and said, "I thought you weren't going to ask me out."

"I wasn't" I replied. "At that moment".

Ryan got up to walk away, but I stopped him.

"Wait" I said quiet yet meekly. "Tell me why.

Why won't you go out with me?"

"Excuse me" responded Ryan.

So, I repeated myself, "Why won't you go out with me? I know you aren't dating anyone, and you said you're not busy today so, why?" I asked, my voice shaky.

Ryan then walked up to me and said harshly, "Did it ever occur to you that I just may not like you? You're like an annoying fly that just keeps buzzing, regardless of how many times I keep swatting at it, it keeps coming back. Did it ever occur to you that I might be trying to kill that fly, that maybe I no longer want to be annoyed? I've dealt with this since kindergarten... kindergarten!!! It's been eleven years, so why don't you just buzz off and die?" he remarked angrily.

When he said this, he'd said everything looking

directly into my eyes; never once did his gaze shift. I knew he was serious, however, all I could do was smile and say that I understood. It hurt so much to smile, but I couldn't give up. In my mind, if I was able to keep smiling, there was yet hope for me to be with him. So, I smiled in his face; he looked at me as though I was peculiar. Then I walked off. This time, I didn't give him the chance to walk off because I felt as though it was my turn.

After school that day, my friends just wouldn't leave me alone. I didn't want to be bothered nor did I want to argue with them about the matter, so I just stayed in the chemistry class sitting idle. That was until a boy came up and talked to me.

"How long do you plan on staying?" he asked.

"I don't know" I said shyly since I didn't know him. I couldn't believe someone was talking to me.

"How do you do it?" he asked.

"Do what?" I said confused.

"You are the persistent one" he said. "Every day you ask him out, and every day you get rejected yet that doesn't stop you. Why?"

I was surprised by the way he worded it and then thought about it and said, "It's just something I want."

"Want?" he repeated quietly. Then he asked, "Why do you want him?"

"He's just different" I responded.

"Yeah, but every day he hurts you" the boy said "So, why keep wanting that?"

Although I still didn't know his name, I thought about what he said carefully then replied, "Well, in life there's a lot of things you want, and it may not be the easiest to get it, but do you give up? Do you stop desiring that thing because it's hard to get?"

"Maybe" the boy said, "No one wants to keep going through

pain purposely, especially when it can be avoided."

"That's true, but all pain has a purpose. It's not like you just go through it without learning something. You have to be willing to suffer." I said slowly but clearly. "I know that sounds weird" I added, "But that's apart of what life brings. You can't avoid it forever."

"Yeah," he said with understanding, "But you could avoid this."

"You're right, I could. However, if I did, I wouldn't be me. I'm not one to give up on things I want." I said and walked out the classroom.

CHAPTER 4

Facing The Truth

When I walked out the classroom I immediately walked home; when I got there, I saw my Cameron exhausted once again. I was just going to let him sleep, but he must've heard my footsteps because he sat up and asked where I had been. I told him I'd been at school, but we could discuss it later because I knew he was tired.

"No." said Cameron. "Seriously, we need to talk"

"What about?" I asked.

"First thing I want to talk about is that idiot. I heard about what he said to you and I'm not going to keep standing for it."

I was surprised my brother heard about it, so I asked him how he found out.

"It doesn't matter" my brother said, but his tone was rising.

"He told you to die."

He said it a second time with more anger and realization.

"He told you to die all because you keep asking him out. And it's not him that's even feeling any pain from it."

"Wait" I said. "You don't know that he's always been honest with me."

"Honest" he responded annoyed, "Honest" he yelled. "You ask him every day, and he rejects you. What pain is that idiot feeling from that? No matter whether it's your birthday or not, he still feels the need to reject you harshly. And I've stood quiet on the sidelines just like you asked, despite the fact of how I've seen how much he is hurting and humiliating you. I stayed quiet because you asked, but him telling my sister to die... I refuse to stay quiet any longer."

Cameron really sounded hurt.

"You're all I have left" he continued. "And if anything happened, especially since that idiot said it, I'd...."

"Silencio." I cut my brother off.

Tears were now streaming down my face.

"I know I said that he hurts me. And I know he told me to die"

"So why him?" Cameron interrupted.

"Because" I began with a very narrow pained smile, "He's different, and I'm persistent."

My voice was starting to break. Cameron said there was no detouring now. I just simply smiled painfully when at the thought of where this conversation was headed. However, it took a totally unexpected turn.

"There's something else I wanted to tell you. I need you to start going back to work" he said firmly.

"Why?" I asked kind of shocked.

My brother couldn't face me when he said it, but he replied, "Tia doesn't want us here anymore."

"Oh," I said a little hurt. "Will we be like before?" I asked.

"No," he responded quickly. "I wont ever let that happen to you again."

"Us" I reminded. "I don't mind if we're together if it

happens, but I refuse to be alone. You're all I have left" I told him.

Cameron hugged me and apologized.

I looked at my brother sternly and seriously. "Promise me, promise me that you won't leave me."

"I can't promise you that" he said. "But I can promise that I won't allow you to go back on the streets."

"Promise me then. I won't stay anywhere you put me if you're not there. I will come and find you." I yelled.

"You still have school and you need to finish that, not to mention college." "Then I won't go" I told him. "I won't go if it gets in the way of keeping us together."

"Tell you what," Cameron started hesitantly, "If you can give up on that idiot, then I'll let you decide if you finish school, and we'll be together."

I was hurt that my brother said that because he knew I couldn't or wouldn't do it. But this just further showed me how much my brother cared for me. He'd rather go through than both of us if it ever came down to it. I was never able to answer my brother. All I could do was cry; cry for the unknown because life always brought us some pain. And I knew I'd have to be ready and persistent through it all.

The next day Cameron and I went to our job to see about the working situation. I had been working here every summer since I was thirteen, along with my brother so we knew it shouldn't be a problem to start working again. As expected, it wasn't a problem; my boss said he had no problem with me working part time and my brother working full-time. After we finished up with the boss, my brother walked out expecting me to follow afterwards, but I didn't because I had to do something first.

"Boss, would it be too much trouble if you gave me extra hours?" I asked.

My boss looked up stern and asked, "Don't you have school?"

"Yeah, but my brother won't mind, and it won't be trouble."

My boss was hesitant at first but said I could work the overnight shift so I could get paid more.

"Thank you" I said to him graciously and walked out.

When I walked out my brother asked what took so long. I told

him that everything was fine. We then began to walk back home.

CHAPTER 5

Who Knew?

Since I began working overnight, it affected my body and school life tremendously. Even though I'm still able to balance both, it's been kind of hard to ask Ryan out and pay attention in class. I guess he must've noticed today because he poked me during class.

"What's wrong?" he asked.

"Nothing" I replied.

Ryan just looked annoyed and said, "You been so sleepy lately, and you asking me out has minimized, why is that?"

"I work" I said honestly, with a minute smile, "So sometimes I'm tired in class".

"As if." said Ryan. "Who'd hire someone as annoying as you?"

I only smiled, then inquired, "Since I'm so annoying, why do you care if I haven't asked you out that much?"

Ryan just stood there quietly staring at me while I stared at him. It felt like an eternity, but in reality, it might've only been five minutes. He finally caught himself and very nonchalantly said,

"I don't care. But that doesn't explain why you've gotten so skinny."

"Oh that," I said a little less optimistic, "Well it...

it's called survival mode."

Ryan only looked confused, but when I opened my mouth to give him clarity, the bell rang so I walked off, or at least I thought.

"Where are you going?" he asked.

"Chemistry" I replied. "It's my last class."

"Yeah, not going to happen, not until you tell me about survival mode." He said.

"Why?" I asked.

"Because I said so." Ryan responded.

"I know, but why? I mean I thought you hated me, so why concern yourself with me?"

He looked confused, then answered,

"You're really annoying, but I don't hate you. You're just.... Your persistency can just be annoying."

"So, you DON'T wish I'd die?" I asked.

"What are you asking that for? I already told you I don't hate you."

"Yeah, I know. But hating me and wanting me to die are two separate things. You could just be acting as a snake" I told him.

All Ryan did was turn then he replied, "I'm not. And I don't want you to die."

His response shocked me, but I still wasn't sure, so I asked, "How do I know?"

"Ugh" Ryan yelled, "Hope, just answer my question. What is survival mode?"

"It's not eating" I explained. "We can't eat for five days; we must train our bodies to it just in case."

"In case of what?" he asked.

"Why?" I asked. "I still don't know why you want to know, so why should I trust you? How do I know you're not *acting* like you care?"

Ryan's gaze suddenly fell upon our hands. He said, "I am holding your hand, aren't I?" and then walked off.

It was then when I realized Ryan wasn't acting, he was genuinely concerned. It was also then that I realized our hands had touched.

On my way to chemistry, I didn't how to feel. I was happy that Ryan was concerned for me, but I didn't know if now was the time. I knew I'd have to keep working and survival mode wouldn't stop. My brother and I needed this; it was something we had to do, especially since I suggested it.

As I entered my classroom, I didn't expect to do anything but pay attention, however that was interrupted.

"So" said the boy, "You haven't felt much pain."

I was confused by his statement, so I just nodded. I

guess he noticed my confusion, because he continued.

"I'm talking about Ryan. You know, him rejecting you."

"Oh" I said. "Yeah, he still rejects me."

"But you don't seem as hurt" said the boy.

"I've just gotten a little too busy to notice." I replied.

I looked at him again and asked, "What's your name?"

"Josh," he said.

"I'm Hope."

"I know" he said. "You bring a lot of that to that boy."

And with that he went back to writing, while I just sat there and stared.

Going home was a little more difficult today, because

I talked to Josh. And my friends, I don't know about them, they're a mess. But I never let that bother me. I was halfway home before I bumped into someone, who happened to be Ryan.

"What are you doing here?" I asked curiously.

Ryan didn't say anything, nor did he look at me. Instead, he shoved a bag of food in my hands. His gesture surprised me, nonetheless, I couldn't accept it.

"I'm sorry, I can't accept this."

Ryan didn't say anything, nor did he reach his hand out to take it back.

I repeated myself but Ryan cut me off and said, "Just eat it, Stern."

I was happy Ryan cared but why? Why now?

"I remember when we were little you hardly ate; you always saved your food. I didn't get it. I still don't get it, but when I asked, you'd say, "Survival was key" then smile. I didn't get it. I hated it because you looked like you were suffering. Even still, I disliked you too much to care, but not now.

Then he extended his hand and said, "Here."

I just looked at him. I opened my mouth to say I couldn't, but he held his hand up, and said, "I'm not asking, I'm telling you."

He was about to walk, but for some odd reason he stopped. He told me quit survival mode. In a genuine tone he said, "There are plenty of people here to take care of you. It's no need to try to do it alone."

After that he did walk off, and so did I. It was time to get ready to go to work.

CHAPTER 6

Our Bond

When I got to work it was extremely hard for me to focus. Not only was my brother breathing down my neck, but I had this temptation right in front of me. I haven't eaten in three and half days, and this food smelled so good. And when I got up to look at it, it looked even better; that's when my stomach started speaking. I haven't done survival mode like this since I was a kid, so I even started to doubt myself. I was reaching to get the food, when I

Autumn Jackson

heard my brother come in. He looked tired, but I could tell he was furious.

"Hope, how long do you plan on doing this?" Cameron asked frustrated.

"What?" I asked innocently.

Then, with his arms extended, he began shouting, "Almost every day I'm getting phone calls about how sleepy you are, and that your work ethic is beginning to slip."

"It's not" I replied, but that only made him more frustrated.

"Quiet. You work from four pm until six am. You're not even resting properly."

"Yes, I am" I said.

"Silenco" mi hermano said. "Por favor. I see you're tired like me, I see you're trying to work just like me. I don't want that. I want you to still be a kid and have fun. Quit trying so hard to grow up" my brother added.

My brother didn't look at me when he said it because he was too hurt.

"But I'm fine," I tried to reassure him. "I'm okay."

My brother then said sarcastically, "That's why you about to eat food, because you're fine?"

"I wasn't..."

"Don't lie to me" my brother yelled. "You know that I hate liars, they bring so much pain. Stupid liars make you believe it will be okay, when it's not. SO, don't you dare lie to me."

Cameron looked me in the eyes, this time I could see his pain.

"Today is your last time working overnight." My brother said.

"What, why?" I asked. "The boss assigned me here."

That was the last straw for him; what I said had just awakened his rage.

"Don't keep lying to me, Hope! Do you think I'm dumb? I know you went back and asked, just like I know you've been taking care of Tia still, when you should be worrying about yourself. You don't think I know that's where half of your checks have been going? How much longer do you plan to lie?" Cameron yelled. "How much longer?" he repeated.

This time I could tell he was more hurt. I hated seeing him like this; however, I still couldn't leave Tia.

"Ella nos necesita" I said. "She's hurt."

"She's hurt? She's hurt?" Cameron said angrily raising his voice. "Ella no nos quiere en su casa, pero ella esta herida? Ha pasado mucho tiempo desde que tuvimos una casa, pero ella cansada o herida?

Siempre tenemos que cuidarnos pero tia cansada! Yo trabajo todos los dias, todo el dia pero nunca me he quejado. You have a good heart and want to help so much, but I'm not you; I can't do it. I won't feel sorry for someone who's doing this to us – yet another person giving up on us. I know that I can't stop you and I'm not trying to hurt you, but just think as to why you're doing this."

"Because she needs help," I said almost immediately. "No one should have to suffer and especially not alone."

"Yet she's putting us out" he said.

He was annoyed because he knew we wouldn't see eye to eye.

"Even still, I can't just watch people suffer, especially after all she has done for us." I said.

"As far as I'm concerned, she's done nothing." After

that he walked off leaving me to work.

CHAPTER 7

Swarms Of Emotion

After me and my brother's argument, we'd been distant. We hadn't talked or seen each other; it was almost as though we had become strangers. Yes, it was true I was still taking care of Tia and still receiving lunch from Ryan. But I never thought that mattered. I never thought something like this would break us apart.

It broke my heart because I couldn't stand losing my

brother. Despite this, I knew there was nothing I could do to align our paths. So, I just walked to school, wondering, *does my brother hate me?* No, he couldn't, but still I was becoming something he couldn't stand. I knew my persistency annoyed him, and my optimistic attitude about the world didn't help. But what made it worse was the fact that I had lied to him, and hid things from him and I knew he hated that. I knew he probably viewed himself as our father, but still I couldn't change.

When I got to school, I saw Ryan, and could tell he was upset. However, that didn't stop me from walking up to him.

"What's wrong?" I asked.

"Nothing" he said annoyed.

"I can tell you're lying" I replied.

"Yeah, well, I can tell you're annoying."

"Just tell me what's wrong" I said.

"I'm not trying to…"

"Just buzz off. Your stupid optimism won't change anything. It makes things worse and confuses me." He yelled.

What he said was a punch to the stomach, yet I had one last question.

"Ryan," I said barely audible, "Will you go out with me?" I asked with so much pain.

He just looked disgusted, then said, "I hate people like you."

"How can you honestly say that?" I asked with a smile that was so close to nonexistent.

Ryan didn't answer, he just walked away, just like my brother did. They both walked away and left me, Ryan my honest friend, and my brother. And it was all because of my persistency, and my optimistic view of the world. It was at that moment I wanted to despise these two characteristics. I wanted to get rid of them so much, but I couldn't. For whatever the reason, I just couldn't. I couldn't stand the thought of losing what made me, me.

And for the first time I cried. I felt no hope, I couldn't smile. I couldn't even understand why my name was Hope. I felt so much despair and pain, all I wanted to do was cry, but crying wasn't enough, so I left. Not knowing someone was watching me.

CHAPTER 8

The Voice

I ended up leaving and walked to a bridge. It was here where people walked back and forth every day. Out of their old troubles and into new ones. It seemed we run to pain. That's all I felt I'd been doing, I had been feeling the pain for so long, but my mind told me there was a third option. There was a way to make this pain end forever.

"You could jump" my mind said. "People do it, and

it's not like you'd be missed. They hate you."

The voice was growing stronger with each minute. "Just do it. Jump, you won't be missed."

Tears began to well in my eyes. *Should I jump?* I thought. *What could I lose? I already lost my brother, and my friend. So, what difference would it make if I jumped?* If I jumped, I wouldn't feel anymore pain. I'd hit the water pretty hard, but besides that jumping didn't seem hard; it was the easy way out. As I got positioned to jump, I heard a voice. It yelled, "Don't do it!"

The voice was masculine. I thought it was Ryan, so I disregarded it. Until they yelled again, "Don't do it!" I looked to see Josh, and he looked scared, but behind him was a even more scared boy. It was Ryan. He looked shocked, and hurt. He walked up to me and grabbed me.

"What do you think you were doing?" He yelled.

I just stayed quiet.

"Answer me" he yelled. "Why? Why would you try do this?"

"Because" I said softly, "Because I couldn't take both of you hating me."

Ryan looked upset, then asked, "That's why?" belittling my reason. "You were going to kill yourself because we're mad at you?" He asked angrily.

"Shut up" I said. "You don't get it. You could never understand how much pain I've been through."

Ryan just took a deep breath and said, "You're probably right, but when have you ever let pain get to you? You're the persistent one."

"Yeah, but I still feel pain just like you. I still get hurt" I said.

The only thing Ryan could do was look away.

Then Josh said, "You're right, you do feel a lot of pain, but you're stronger than most. Most people could never have gone through what you went through, and still persevere through it. And this is your first time getting knocked off the road...and you've always stayed true to yourself."

His words made me feel a little better, but I still felt this pain. "They still hate me, the people I need hate me." I uttered.

Josh then went eye level with me, and said, "YOU need you. You need you first, you need to be okay with you. You live for you, no matter what. Don't let people detour you, you understand?"

It was at that moment, I felt such a weight being lifted off my chest, even still I couldn't help but cry.

"Promise" said Josh, "Promise you'll always live for

you, no matter what."

"I promise" I said through tears.

"Not like that – you must mean it when you say it" said Josh.

"I promise" I said louder.

"I can't feel your hope" exclaimed Josh.

It was then I started crying so much harder, but this time I was able to smile with it. "I promise" I said wiping my eyes. "I promise."

"Good" Josh said, then looked at Ryan. "Take care of her" and with that he left leaving me there with Ryan.

It was awhile before I stopped crying, and an even longer while before me and Ryan left. I didn't know what to say to him. I was tired and just wanted to go home. But he wasn't ready yet; not once did he ever look at me. It was like he was there, but not mentally and I didn't like seeing him like that, so I asked how'd he find me. It took him a moment to answer, but eventually he said "Josh", and began to explain.

"When I walked off and left earlier, Josh immediately came to find me, he made me come. He knew something was wrong, but I didn't listen. I was upset about something else, so Josh ended up dragging me.

"Why you? Why'd Josh get you?"

"Don't really know" responded Ryan, "Could be because I was the one who always rejected you, or maybe because I pushed you to go this far. Or maybe, maybe that idiot still knows his best friend" said Ryan slowly.

"What?" I said confused. "I've never seen you guys together."

"That's because we aren't now" explained Ryan. "He was my best friend until fifth grade, but then he started getting annoying, so I cut him off. Even through all that, he still cared about me, he still cared." said Ryan softly. He then looked at me and said, "You know he may be the reason I started disliking you more. That persistency, you both had it and it was strong. I had already got rid of one, but for some reason I couldn't stand the thought of losing another", Ryan said.

With that, we began to walk to my house.

CHAPTER 9

Our Story

Surprisingly when I entered my house, I saw my brother, and he was exhausted. Nevertheless, my brother still got up to greet me, but was surprised by Ryan. He looked puzzled, then asked, "What's the idiot doing here?"

"He walked me home" I said.

"Why?"

But I just shrugged him off, no longer wanting to

talk. My brother noticed the shift in my attitude and said, "The food is ready if you're eating."

Cameron knew I wasn't going to eat, not like this, but he didn't want to cause a scene in front of Ryan.

So, I said, "I'm going to my room" leaving him alone with Ryan.

Cameron told me that Ryan just stared, watching me go up the stairs. He said it was annoying but ultimately invited him to stay for dinner and Ryan accepted.

"Aren't you going to go get Hope?"

"Nope" Cameron replied. "It's no point of talking to her when she's like that."

That must've made Ryan mad because he yelled, "She almost DIED today! She tried to kill herself." Ryan explained.

When Cameron heard him say that, his heart sunk, but he wasn't going to let this punk see that.

"Did she?" Cameron asked.

"Yeah" Ryan remarked sadly.

"Well, honestly, I'm surprised it hasn't happened sooner."

"WHAT?" yelled Ryan furiously. "You *expected* your sister might do this and you didn't even care? You KNEW she might've killed herself and you chose to do nothing? You really are a horrible brother."

"At that point" Cameron told me, "I punched the stupid twerp. and told him that he knew nothing about me or you. I looked him in the eyes, and explained how much we had been through. I told him how I hated him and that the only reason I tolerated him is because of you."

"So, don't you dare try to tell me how bad a person I am, when we both have brought her nothing but pain." He told Ryan.

"But you knew", croaked Ryan, "You knew she might've done this."

I then looked up at the ceiling and said no, I just knew it might happen and begin to tell our story...

When we were little, we always stayed with our dad. We didn't even know our mom for a while, but that was okay because we had each other, and that was enough. But then one day our dad couldn't handle us, and said he needed some space, so he took us to our mom. By that time, I was six, and Hope was three. I didn't know what to expect from my mother, since I had never known her, but I was hopeful. When we first arrived, I remember being so excited, and cheerful because I was finally meeting my mother.

However, that was quickly replaced when I seen how stern and poor my mom was.

Often times there wasn't enough to eat, so me and Hope always shared. We weren't full, but it was sufficient. Our clothes were never clean, but Hope and I didn't mind. We didn't mind that Mom didn't have hot water to bathe us, nor did she always have soap. We were okay with everything because we were together, we had a family.

All that changed though, after three months because Mom said she couldn't provide for us and kicked us out. We stayed on the streets and lived in a box. Times were so hard, but at first bearable because people would feed or clothe us. But eventually that stopped; they stopped caring once they saw the begging wouldn't stop. I got so scared and desperate. The garbage cans even stopped being filled, and as time went on my sister and I almost hadn't eaten in a month. And I remember telling her that we'd have to steal. But Hope wouldn't stand for it.

She just told me we couldn't, and there was another way. And I remember yelling at her telling her no one wanted to care for us, and that we'd die if we didn't steal. But she just shook her head and said there's another way. And everyday she'd go to people's door knocking asking for help. People got annoyed by her, and so they gave her a nickname, The One, The Persistent One. Even though my sister annoyed the crap out of people or was often ignored, she never stopped.

That went on for two years, and eventually I joined her. One day however, we were sleeping in our box like usual and a man found us, and he took us on a plane. That man was my father; he had finally come back, and I thought he'd take care of us, but he didn't. He flew us to Illinois to stay with Tia, then left. Never once did he say anything to us. Tia took care of us enough to get through school, but she still required that we work and buy our own food, which I was fine with, since I was tired of relying on people.

However, school for us was hard. We were behind two years, and on top of that we didn't speak English since we're from Mexico. Although my sister had it worse because people would laugh at our language, and your rejections didn't help. She used to hate the language, and feel so alone, but the language was what brought us closer together.

"Didn't you get bullied too?" Ryan asked.

"No, I stood up for myself, and I would've done the same for my sister but she asked me not to. She didn't like the way I handled things, she said I was too violent."

"Oh, that's why you never hurt me. I always thought you were just weak." Ryan replied.

"No, trust me, I wanted to kill you, but my sister would always change my mind." Cameron responded.

"I can imagine" said Ryan.

Then the room fell quiet, and Cameron went to the kitchen to get the pasta.

"Can't she eat with us?" Ryan asked.

"If you can get her."

CHAPTER 10

The Date

I had been in my room with my pajamas on for like twenty minutes; I was hungry, but didn't feel like eating. I just couldn't believe that I almost did that, that I'd almost killed myself. I was slowly brought back into reality when I heard a knock on my door.

"Can I come in the voice said?"

By then I knew it was Ryan because my brother never

knocked. I opened the door slowly and said, "What is it you want?"

He then took it upon himself to let himself in and scan my room.

"It's plain" he said surprised.

"Yeah," I said. "Never know when we might leave so I don't decorate."

"But you're the complete opposite of this." he said.

"What does that mean?" I felt my face burning up.

Ryan noticed it then smirked, and said, "That's cute, but I still don't like you."

"I never said that" I responded flustered.

"I know" said Ryan, "but I would like it if you ate with us."

My head was beginning to hurt, and I wasn't sure why, however that didn't stop me from backing away.

"I'm not hungry" I said.

"And you weren't hungry when I gave you those lunches either" Ryan replied. "This is a one-time thing; I'm asking you out, so consider this a date."

I felt myself begin to smile, but then said, "I'm in my pajamas."

"So, what" he responded. "Just be you."

With that he guided me down the stairs to the dinner table.

Me and Ryan both sat across from my brother, making lots of jokes and laughing. My brother just observed us; it went for awhile like this, before my brother spoke and said, "I guess he's not a complete idiot."

I looked up and smiled and said, "Nope, I told you he was different."

"But you never told me why" responded Cameron.

"Yeah, me either" chimed Ryan.

"It's because of what he did for us in Mexico." I stated.

"What?" my brother replied. "I don't remember this."

"That's because on this day, we went on separate walks looking for food and I bumped into him. Even though he was still a kid, I asked for his help, and he was the first one in a long time to treat me like a person. He walked around with me and bought us lots of food; he even introduced me to his dad, Robert. I was so grateful to him, because I hadn't seen that type of kindness in a long time and thought it was dying out." I then looked at Ryan and said, "You're the reason I'm so optimistic toward the world, and never quit my persistency."

"Wait a minute" said my brother, "I remember that day you came home with lots of food – enough for two weeks!"

"Yep" I said.

Ryan then realized, "You're *that* girl? The one I asked to go home with us?"

"Yeah, you finally remember."

"What?" yelled my brother.

"She didn't come though," Ryan said slowly. "She said it was because she couldn't leave her brother."

Ryan looked at my brother then me. "We were those same little kids from back then. With such different stories and lives" he said. "You're that girl. You're the little girl. Well, you're not even little anymore, you're actually a girl."

And from that moment forward, the way Ryan viewed me was different. We both stared at each other, but it didn't last long because of my brother.

"All right, that's it." Cameron stated. "I want him gone. He's been here long enough.

"But I haven't finished my spaghetti" Ryan objected.

"Take it with you" said my brother before he pushed him out the house.

"You didn't have to be so mean; he was just eating." I said.

"Yeah well, he ate enough" Cameron replied.

"But I wanted him to stay a little while longer."

"Too bad" he said and then walked off.

He came back to tell me he had to go to work, which left me to think of everything that just happened.

CHAPTER 11

A Familiar Face

The following day going to school felt completely weird and different for me, and that was because Ryan was different. Not only was he nicer to me, but he also started being back friends with Josh. It wasn't like I was upset, I just hadn't expected it. However, no good thing lasts forever, because today, a familiar face joined our class. Zabrina was Ryan's ex-girlfriend (his first love); they were always off and on, that was until she moved. That was when Ryan stopped dating, but now she back.

I could only look at him, as I felt Josh look at me. I could tell he was concerned, but I simply smiled his way (it wasn't strong, but it'd suffice). I knew Ryan still felt emotions towards her, that part was evident, but it was almost like he didn't want to. It made me wonder why, I knew he still didn't like me even though now, he viewed me as a girl. So why, I thought, why stop yourself from dating? But I'd never find out, especially now, because Zabrina was walking his way.

"Ryan," she yelled, "I missed you! It's been so long."

Ryan could only turn his head, but I could tell by the look on his face, he missed her too. It went on all day like that, Ryan ignoring Zabrina, but Zabrina stopped. She looked like me I thought, but the only difference here was I knew Ryan. He liked Zabrina, I knew he was hurt so he'd try to keep his distance, but it'd only be so long, I could tell. Regardless of this, I refused to give up on Ryan; he wasn't dating Zabrina yet, so I knew there still was a chance.

"A chance" I said as I smiled, but this time it was weaker.

"You okay? asked Josh.

"Yeah. I'm not giving up." I replied.

Josh only laughed then said, "Don't get hurt."

After that he walked off.

"I won't" I said.

Time had been flying very quickly for me, and it was never a bore. It had become quite hard to keep Ryan's attention since Zabrina was always around. But I couldn't be too upset because I had been working a lot. And besides, Ryan was coming over to hang out today. He still felt like I wasn't eating enough, and he was right, but I wouldn't tell him. I was happy though, because life had been so good for me, and I planned on it staying like that.

The day couldn't have been longer, classes took forever to end, and Ryan took forever to come. I already knew why it was because he still really liked Zabrina. It pained me to see him with her, but I still wanted to see him happy, so I wouldn't oppose. When Ryan finally got to my locker, he apologized and asked if I was ready.

"Yeah," I smiled, and then we were off.

It didn't take long before we got to Tia's house, but once we did, I was wishing we hadn't. Tia was home, and she was sitting on the couch expecting us.

"Where've you been?" she asked.

"Nowhere," I responded. "School and work."

"Well, if you're at work, why is there never any food here?" Her voice was raising and becoming more demanding.

"We, we have to save" I replied. "You said you..."

"How dare you live in MY house and think you're not going to do anything, while bringing other people here? I want you out!" Tia screamed.

My mouth just gaped. "You're not serious?" I asked.

But she was.

"Out now" she yelled.

That was when my brother walked in, and I knew he was tired. He could feel the atmosphere was tense and could tell Tia was upset. He just looked at me, then Ryan and told her we'd be gone by tonight. After that he didn't say another word, he just walked up the stairs to pack his things. I was about to do the same until I looked at Ryan. He had so much worry and fear in his eyes. So, I stayed and talked to him to let him know it would be alright. Afterwards, I hugged him and he never let go for fear if he had, he'd lose me.

Ryan never left, even later in that day, and my brother and I had our things.

"Where are you going to go?" Ryan asked.

I just shrugged, but my brother said, "I've got a friend."

Ryan just shook his head, then said, "At least let me take you two to dinner."

I turned to my brother who turned his head as well, but then said, "You two go."

Shocked at what my brother said, I turned my head and asked if he was serious.

"Yeah," he said. "I got some stuff to handle anyways."

Ryan only looked at him then said, "It's only right you come too."

"No thanks" my brother said. He then threw me some cash. "Here, this will cover you."

I could only look at him with astonishment in my eyes, and said, "I can't just…"

"Bye. Just go. And bring her back at eleven", he yelled to Ryan. I turned to look at him as well as Ryan, but neither of us spoke a word. We both just left.

As we exited the house Ryan asked where I wanted to eat? I told him that it didn't matter, anywhere would be fine.

"No" said Ryan. "It's your night, so you choose."

I thought for a moment, then said, "I don't know, I guess Walmart or an Aldi's is would be fine."

"What?" said Ryan laughing, "I mean like a restaurant."

At that moment I could only turn my head. "I don't know any," I said honestly.

"What?" asked Ryan. "Haven't you ever eaten a burger or chicken or anything!?"

"No" I responded. "We've never had enough money to splurge like that, so I wouldn't know."

"Really? What about ice cream or cookies or pop?"

"Nope. We don't waste money on unnecessary things, but I have had Macaroni before. Not often, but we've had it." I say proudly.

Ryan just looked shocked, and said, "You're serious?"

"Well, yeah," I said. "Tia never took us anywhere, and it's always been up to my brother to provide for us, so we eat a lot of pasta."

Ryan could only look away, as though he had pity for me.

"Don't look like that," I said with a smile. "It's not all bad, I mean we're not hungry, and we're grateful for every meal."

"You're really different, you know that, right?" Ryan remarked.

"Yeah" I smiled.

Ryan then stated, "I know where we're going."

And with that we were off walking.

When we arrived, my eyes immediately enlarged. I had never seen so many different foods or drinks in the same place. Ryan couldn't stop laughing, but nevertheless he paid for both meals, then asked what I wanted to try first? I didn't know (I was still amazed at all the different foods).

Ryan took my hand and said, "C'mon."

I had so many different foods: pizza, chicken, tacos, burgers and so much more. And there were all sorts of breads and desserts, all I could do was smile.

"The only thing that could make this better, was if my brother

were able to try it," I said.

"Already got it" said Ryan.

"Really?" I asked shocked. "Oh, here" I said while handing Ryan the money for me.

"Don't worry about it" Ryan said.

"Yeah, but..."

"Keep it, Hope" Ryan said, his tone serious. "You know you can trust me, right?"

"Yeah" I responded.

"And you know you can lean and depend on me for anything right? he asked more sternly.

But I didn't look at him. "Yeah" I answered.

Ryan then grabbed my face and said, "I'm serious,

Hope. You can depend on me."

But when he said that, my heart began to shake, I just didn't know. He had Zabrina, and it wouldn't be just one person but two of us. Thinking of it from a rational perspective, it just didn't make sense. Nevertheless, I smiled and told him okay. After that we left.

CHAPTER 12

A New Start

Ryan had dropped me off just like my brother told him, but I still ended up having to wait for Cameron. It took awhile for my brother to finally show up, but he did, and he was with Joaquin Stone. That was my brother's best friend since kid years, I never really trusted him though; he always seemed like a troublemaker.

He came up to me and said, "What up, Hope?"

I just turned my head.

"Still stubborn I see" Joaquin said.

My brother glared at me.

"Fine" I muttered to my brother.

"So, how long y'all plan on staying?" asked Joaquin.

"Not long, hopefully no longer than three months, six at the most." Cameron replied.

"What?" I asked shocked. "That long? But what about..."

But my brother only silenced me with his glare.

"Okay" said Joaquin. "I'm fine with it, but you do know y'all will have to pay half the rent, and bills, along with your own food."

My brother just shook his head in approval, and we were off to our temporary home.

The past few days had been nothing but punishment

for me. I didn't like the house we lived in because it was really small and cramped and had so many rules. I could tell the people around me weren't happy, so it was hard to smile. My brother was constantly working, and Ryan had his own problems with his life. I knew he wanted to check up on me, but that made things complicated for him, which I didn't want. So, it's just been me and Josh lately, but even with that, he was still hardly around. He wanted to be a friend for Ryan, which was understandable. I just wish somewhere I could see smiles.

As I walked into class, I saw Ryan and Zabrina arguing again. This had become a routine, and I was pretty sure I knew why. Despite this, I walked over and greeted them with a smile, but my response was anger and irritation from the both of them. Josh immediately came and dragged me away and asked how everything was going at home? I just shrugged.

He said I hadn't been smiling much. I then turned my head towards Ryan and Zabrina.

Josh took a deep breath and said, "You're really going to let them make you stop smiling?"

"No" I said quickly. "It's just a lot."

"There's always going to be a lot, but you can't let that take away your joy" remarked Josh.

I smiled and said, "You're right", but no sooner I said that we both saw a raging Ryan coming over. When he got to us, he snatched Josh and said, "We got to go."

Once Josh and Ryan were out of ear shot, Ryan began talking.

"I need a favor" said Ryan.

"Which is?" asked Josh.

"Keep Zabrina busy today."

Josh only looked confused and asked, "Why?"

"Because I need to check up on Hope; besides I gave Hope my word last week."

"So, tell Zabrina that" Josh said simply.

"I can't" shouted Ryan. "I can't" he said more conflicted. "Look, I just need to know if you'll help."

"I will" said Josh, but after this, this has to stop.

"Excuse me?" Ryan exclaimed.

"It's time to choose and let them both know. The way your doing it is not only hurting both of them, but it's going to cause you to lose both of them as well." Josh explained.

"I'm not asking for your love advice" Ryan said harshly.

"Neither am I" responded Josh. "But in either case, I'm not going to help you hurt Hope."

After that Josh walked off.

CHAPTER 13

Figuring Things Out

At first, leaving from school felt pretty lonely. However, the feeling soon went away because I was met by Ryan.

"So, how've you been?" He asked.

"Same" I said.

Ryan then studied me and said, "You're lying. You live in a new place. How's that been? Where do you even live?"

"My brother's friend and it's definitely been something" I said flatly.

Ryan stopped me in my tracks and asked, "What's wrong?"

"Nothing" I said, but I failed to make eye contact.

"Don't lie to me, Hope." said Ryan more seriously. "What's wrong?"

"Don't you have Zabrina? Shouldn't you be with her? I frustratedly responded.

"Why are you getting upset?" Ryan asked. "Zabrina's not my girlfriend, so I can go anywhere I want."

"Yeah, well not with me. I'm going home."

Ryan got in my way, refusing to move.

"Move" I told Ryan, but he didn't. "Move" I said a

little louder.

Not only did he not move but he walked closer to me. And for some reason I got upset and started yelling, "Move, *Move*, MOVE!!!" I started hitting his chest, but he never did move.

Ryan grabbed my hands and asked, "Hope, what's wrong? Don't lie either because I know something's wrong."

I honestly replied, "I don't feel comfortable at home, I don't feel like I have any privacy and my brother is never there to protect me. I don't want to make us lose our house, but I don't want to kiss him." I said with tears in my eyes.

"Kiss who?" asked Ryan.

"Joaquin. He's been coming on a lot more since my brother been gone. And if I don't, I know we won't have anyway to live." I explained.

Ryan then balled up his fist and started to walk because he was upset.

"Where are you going?" I asked.

"To see him" Ryan said.

"No, you can't." I shouted. I grabbed his arm and repeated, "You can't."

"Then, I'm telling your brother" said Ryan.

I only shook my head with a smile and tears falling from my eyes.

"Hope? Why not?" Ryan yelled.

"We wouldn't have anywhere to stay, besides, Joaquin is really not a bad person. I learned that he really does care for my brother." I explained.

"Yeah, but what about you?" asked Ryan.

I smiled and said, "He hasn't done anything to me thus far."

Ryan only glanced at me and could tell I was lying.

"We need to tell someone" Ryan insisted.

"I did" I said lowly.

"Who?" asked Ryan.

"Josh."

"Josh?" said Ryan confused. He stared at me then said, "C'mon."

"Where are we going?" I asked.

"I'm taking you home" Ryan said.

With that we began walking.

The whole walk home Ryan didn't say anything to me, he just looked forward.

"So, are you upset with me?" I asked.

"No" replied Ryan flatly.

But he didn't look at me.

"What did I do wrong?" I asked.

"Nothing" he said. "Now, leave it be."

I thought for a moment and said, "This is because of the Josh thing, isn't it?"

"No" said Ryan offensively.

"Why are you getting upset? It's not like..."

Ryan stopped walking, then faced me. "How could you tell him first? I mean honestly, you've known and liked me *first*, so why would you tell him?"

"He was there. You were with Zabrina so..."

"SO, you just didn't tell me?" Ryan interrupted.

"NO" I said and then took a step back, no longer feeling safe. "I don't see a problem."

"The problem" said Ryan, "is you're not relying on me. You've wanted me for years, and now I'm giving myself to you, and UGHH."

He then swung at the air; I could feel the breeze against my face. I took a breath and said, "I got to go."

Ryan started to reach out, he started to speak, but he didn't.

I continued home by myself.

When I got home, I was hoping to be by myself and just rest for a while. However, my dreams didn't coming true, because Joaquin was here.

"That was a quite a commotion you and your boyfriend just caused" said Joaquin.

"He's not my boyfriend" I replied.

"Good" said Joaquin. "Nice to see you know who you belong to."

He then started walking closer towards me as I backed away. I backed away until there was nowhere to go, and even then, I still tried to run, that was until Joaquin finally caught me. Then he asked, "Why you being like this?" His grip around my waist began to tighten as I pulled away.

"So today's the day that you finally kiss me" he said.

I began to start resisting more and yelling for him to stop.

"Shut up" he said, "I'm not even doing anything."

But before he could go any further, my brother walked in.

"Hope, is that you?" he asked. His eyes glanced around first, but once his eyes focused on us, Cameron was no longer calm and soft; he was enraged.

CHAPTER 14

Another Change

My brother looked at us for a moment, then said, "What are you doing? Get off my sister!"

Joaquin quickly stepped back and said, "Chill man, we always play like this."

"Play? Play! My sister not your play toy." Cameron hollered.

"Chill out" said Joaquin. "We weren't doing anything."

My brother didn't believe him. He looked at me and asked, "What was he about to do?"

I didn't answer, so my brother asked again angrier and more serious this time. I still didn't respond so my brother yelled, "Hope Amelia Stern, if you don't answer my question, I'll..."

"He tried to kiss me" I said slowly, and low.

My brother was getting more upset. "How long?"

"I didn't" said Joaquin, although my brother ignored him.

"How long?" Cameron asked me again.

Joaquin was looking at me shaking his head. I answered anyway and said, "A week after we got here."

My brother then slammed his hands against the table. "We've been here for a month, a month. Why hadn't you said anything?"

I didn't answer.

"Why?" he yelled.

I couldn't answer; I just started crying.

My brother looked at Joaquin, and asked, "What else have you tried to do to my sister?"

Joaquin said, "Dude, chill. This ain't even real; it's all just a joke." He looked at me for confirmation, but I didn't look up.

My brother did however, and said, "Don't even look at my sister. You're a disgusting creature."

Joaquin said, "Oh really? Well, if I'm so disgusting, I guess your sister is too, because I do nothing but hug all day when she get's home."

Cameron went up to Joaquin and punched him, it wasn't just any punch either – it was in his face.

Joaquin then felt his face and felt a bloody lip and nose.

"Get out" he yelled.

I guess neither me nor my brother comprehended what he said because neither one of us moved.

"I said get out" Joaquin repeated himself, more seriously. "Back to the streets, where you belong" he then added.

My brother was angry, but nonetheless he grabbed our things so we could leave. As we were exiting, I saw him put something on the table.

"What was that?" I asked.

"Our rent" he said annoyed.

"But why?" I asked.

"Because" he said, "you taught me, we should always do right by people."

After that we left searching for a new home.

We had been looking for awhile for our new house, but sadly everything was so expensive. And it started to get hard for my brother to work. So, we found ourselves where we first started, in a box. The only difference this time was we weren't hungry yet. We had food.

It had been awhile since it was just me and my brother, but I was grateful because it could've been worse.

As we entered our box today my brother said, "I'm sorry."

"Why?" I asked.

"Because we're here in this same predicament again, and I couldn't stop it."

Autumn Jackson

"It's fine" I said. "I don't blame you."

"But you haven't been able to go to school in a week" my brother said.

"But you wanted it that way" I said. "I would've gone."

"They would've teased you" he responded.

"So. Let them. It's not like they haven't before; besides, as long as I got you, I don't really care what anyone says."

My brother then took a breath and I placed my head on his shoulder.

And out of nowhere he said, "Why didn't you tell?"

He was referring to Joaquin and I knew it, but I didn't know how to answer his question or more like, I didn't want to.

"I don't know" I said slowly. I then took another deep

breath and said, "Maybe it was because I didn't want us to lose the house, or for you to blame yourself for this. Or maybe, I didn't want for you to lose your friend" I said hesitantly. "You had to grow up so fast, and missed so much, but Joaquin always made you laugh and feel like a boy. You never felt the need to act grown up around him; you would just be you. And I didn't want you to lose that. I didn't want you to lose your last piece of childhood."

My brother only smiled at me, and said, "That's nice, but everyone has to grow up, Sis. You can't be a child forever. Your needs change."

I looked confused.

"So, if I was to always play, now as a man, I wouldn't get any work done, and I couldn't take care of you. It's different when you're a child because a child's job is to play. There's a time and a place, and as you get older what you need and what you want are different."

I just began to think on what my brother said. How, as I get older, things I want and need change. I thought it'd be complicated, but it wasn't. I then looked at my brother and I analyzed myself, it was then I knew change was coming.

CHAPTER 15

Our Relationship

After a week of not being in school I finally returned, but I wasn't smelling the best. Josh first seen me and gave me a look. I, in turn nodded, leaning to him to pass me a spare shirt and soap. Not too long after that I freshened myself up in the bathroom, then I walked in the classroom. And the first one to greet me was Ryan!

"Where have you been?" he asked. "You just ditched

school and didn't say anything?"

"Sorry" I said. "It won't happen again."

And sure, enough it hadn't. But what happened with Ryan and Zabrina? Even though they'd never admit it, I was pretty sure Ryan was the one who wanted to keep it a secret. But he did a bad job at hiding it, or maybe it's just because I could tell he was happier. Even so, Ryan still tried to spend a lot of time with me, which I didn't think was good.

"So, when can I come over again?" he asked.

I just looked at him and said, "I don't think that's a good idea, I mean you have Zabrina now."

"She's fine with it" said Ryan.

I then turned my head towards Zabrina, and she looked anything but fine.

"Trust me" said Ryan, with a reassuring voice, "she's okay with it."

"Even still, I said hesistantly, "now wouldn't be a good time."

"Why not?" asked Ryan concerned. "Is it because of Joaquin?"

"NO" I said.

"Then why?" asked Ryan.

However, I didn't tell him, I just walked away. I realized it might've been mean for me to just walk away from Ryan, but I still hadn't told him. Honestly, I didn't know how or even if I should, I mean it was my problem. All of my thinking led me to walking without paying attention, which resulted in me bumping into Josh. At first, he looked upset, but then once he realized it was me, concern immediately fell into his eyes.

"Hope" he said gently, "What's wrong?"

I only shook my head and said, "I don't know."

This made Josh try and guess my problem. "Is it Ryan? Does seeing him with Zabrina hurt?"

In all honest truth it did still hurt, just not as much, so I nodded to Josh. However, he wasn't satisfied with my answer.

"What else is it then?" he inquired.

I could only turn my head from him, then said, "I don't know" with a shaky voice.

At this point, Josh wasn't saying anything, he was completely silent, and I hated the silence.

So, I asked, "Aren't you going to say anything?"

He just shook his head in disapproval though, and said, You just lied to me. So, whatever this is you don't feel comfortable telling me... I'm fine with that" he said with a smile.

He smiled I thought, and it wasn't a small one either. His was big, and vibrant with so much hope. It was like he was screaming, "It'll only get better".

I then took a breath and said, "I don't have anywhere to go."

"So, my guess was right" said Josh. "I thought it was weird you hadn't been here. And then when you came back, it's like you were telling a story."

I nodded.

"Why hadn't you told any of us sooner?" he asked. "We would've helped."

"It would've complicated a lot of things" I said, as I took a breath and hugged my knees.

"Even me?" questioned Josh. "I get Ryan, but why me?"

"I didn't want to complicate or ruin your friendship. You're both stubborn and adding me to the mix would've been turmoil."

"You still care for him, huh?" remarked Josh flatly.

"Yeah" I said weakly. "I can't help it."

Josh then said, "You're a good friend."

"So are you" I replied.

And we both just ended up sitting in the hallway waiting for school to end.

CHAPTER 16

Proposal

School ended rather quickly, so I went home and so did Josh. He understood my reasoning, so he wasn't upset, maybe a little hurt, but not angry. Regardless, neither one of us would talk about it again, there was no need.

As I began to walk home, I started to feel faint. That was to be expected seeing as how I hadn't eaten in four days, and straining my brain like this didn't help.

Autumn Jackson

Nevertheless, I kept on walking home, and when I got there I was greeted with a surprise. My brother was smiling genuinely, and it had been a long time since he'd done that. I asked, "What happened?"

My brother said, "I finally believe you. You know when you say everything will be alright."

"Really?" I responded. "And what made you believe me?"

"I went to work and not only did they have work for me, but you as well." He explained.

"Really?" I said shocked.

Cameron simply nodded, and told me that the boss had a proposition for us.

"Which is what?" I asked.

"He offered to take us in."

"Hugh!!!!" I shrieked in amazement.

"I know and believe me I've thought about it. But I don't want to do it if you feel uncomfortable. I made that mistake once, even though I want to protect you, it does no good for me if it's not what you want. So how do you feel? Do you know what you want?" he asked.

"I do" I said, "but first I need to know why. Why him? Why not try to go back to Tia? I asked.

My brother looked at the sky and said, "The boss, he cares. He was concerned where'd we gone the last two weeks, and why I looked the way I did. I came prepared to beg, even kneel for a job if I had to, so I could take care of you. Pathetic, right? But the boss wouldn't allow me. In fact, when he seen me, he treated me like family. Or at least what I remember family being" said my brother.

He hugged me and was genuinely concerned. "Tia never once hugged us, nor did or does she miss us.

We... I can't go back to that" said my brother. "His offer may be a good thing in disguise."

Cameron's response only confirmed my answer; I had never heard him talk about family. Especially not in regard to anyone else. "So" I said, "When do we leave?"

My brother simply looked at me with shock, and asked, "Are you going to come with me?"

"Of course, you're my brother." I smiled and he smiled too.

He told me we'd have to wait a week.

"That's okay; I have no problem waiting." I responded.

We both sat there waiting for the week to pass by. I had gone to school the next week, but just barely. I had only gone two days (Monday and Wednesday) and neither day did I really talk. I just said a few words to Ryan and Josh, then I was gone. I hadn't specifically told them where, but they knew I'd be back, although I got word that Ryan had been worried...

It's the end of the week now and Hope still hasn't shown. I would've called, but she doesn't have a phone. And I have no idea where she lived, or why she was trying to keep me away. I then got an idea that maybe Josh might know. I saw Josh when he walked pass me, then walked over to him.

"Yo" I hollered out.

"What?" Josh responded.

"Where is she? And don't bother lying because I know you know."

Josh then looked up surprised and questioned, "You don't?"

I grabbed Josh's shirt and said, "Stop fooling

around."

But Josh quickly snatched away and asked what was my problem? I felt a fury break in me and said, "What's wrong with me? It's you! How could I know, when now she's all buddy buddy with you? She's...she's ugh, she liked me for years but now treats us as equals" I said defeated while taking a seat.

Josh then sat beside me and said, "I'm not trying to steal her; I'm just trying to be a good friend."

"Naw" said Ryan with realization, "She's in good hands. You just take care of her."

Josh looked at me weird.

"But I do need to know where she is" I reiterated more seriously this time.

Josh only took a breath and said, "I'm not exactly sure, she won't tell me all that. All I know is that she's homeless."

Before I knew it, I was gone.

Autumn Jackson

CHAPTER 17

A Lasting Effect

How could I have not noticed sooner, I thought. *She's homeless, Hope is homeless and I never knew!* I wasn't sure where my legs were taking me, but I wouldn't stop. Before long, I ended up at Tia's house; she was there sitting on the porch.

I quickly walked up to her and asked, "Do you know where Hope is?"

She ignored me, so I asked again, this time more frantically. "Where's Hope?"

Tia quickly looked me over and asked, "Aren't you the one who hurt Hope for years?"

I nodded slowly.

She turned her head from me and said coldly, "I don't know, and if I did know I wouldn't tell you."

"Why?" I asked hurt and confused.

"You hurt her" she said, "I hurt'em too, so the least I can do is keep them away from some pain."

"But I care now, we're real good friends."

She looked me in my eyes sternly. I couldn't tell if she thought I was lying or not. But then she got up and reached for a piece of paper and said, "Here." It had an address on there.

"Thank you" I said and then I was off.

Tia had only nodded and said, "I want to try to do something right."

I couldn't focus on that because I had yet to find Hope. I walked really quickly to this unknown house and immediately starting banging on the door. Some man eventually came out and he reeked of alcohol, nonetheless I asked, "Is Hope here?"

The man hiccupped and said, "They're long gone." He then gave me a smile of despair and said, "I lost my best friend" as he shook his head.

I then knew this was Joaquin. I hated him, but for some odd reason I couldn't be mean to him.

"Do you have any idea where they went?"

"Nope" said Joaquin, with his head low. "Somewhere on the streets I suppose."

I then got an idea and told him thanks. But before I left, I told Joaquin to keep trying to talk to her brother. "Hope's real forgiving and I know her brother can be too, you just got to keep trying."

"Why?" he asked.

"They're the persistent ones, and if you want to be around them, you're going to have to learn to be persistent too."

After that I was off, to one last stop to find Hope.

I arrived at the train station a little after four and began my search for Hope. I remember when she was little, she told me that she liked trains because she believed her family would always come back that way. She used to always come here for hours.

This was my last hope; if Hope wasn't here, I wouldn't know where to go or what I'd do, or if I'd ever seen her again. So, I looked, I looked and gazed for caramel skin with hazel eyes or even curly, long brown hair. Anything to show me Hope was alive, but

I saw nothing. I kept walking and glanced some more, yet to find anything. I then sat down with a look of despair on my face.

That was until I heard a voice, "What's wrong?" it asked.

I had yet to look up though.

"What's wrong?" the voice then asked again.

The voice was feminine, however I wasn't in tune to how it really sounded, so I continued to ignore it. That was until the person started poking me.

"Hope" I then yelled unconsciously, "would you stop..." Then it hit me. "Hope, is that really you?"

"Yeah" she nodded, "who else would it be?"

I then grabbed her and squeezed her for dear life, and asked where she had been.

Hope then looked confused and said, "I've been at school."

I then looked at her, knowing she was lying.

"I've been spending time with my brother and the person we're going to live with. We didn't want it to be awkward."

"Bu,t why not just ask me?" Ryan inquired. "I've got plenty of space for the both of you."

I just shook my head and said, "You've got Zabrina."

To which Ryan replied, "She won't mind."

I only looked at him.

Then he asked, "Don't you still like me? This could be what you wanted."

I was taken aback by what he said, nonetheless I still answered. "Yeah, I like you, but you don't honestly like me. You'd only date me out of pity, just to keep me here and I don't want that."

Ryan then opened his mouth to speak but I stopped

him.

"The way you look at us" I told Ryan, "it's completely different. Mines is in a protective way, and Zabrina, well, you love her."

It didn't hurt anymore to say or see them together, because I was fine with us being friends. I was fine with the way everything was.

Ryan didn't object to what I was saying, he just simply asked, "Where will you go?" His eyes looked so sad and defeated.

I smiled his way. "Don't worry" I said cheerfully. "I'm not going anywhere; for now, everything will be the same. Me and my brother just have to take the train a little way to get to our home, but I'm not leaving our school" I explained.

"Everything will be alright?" asked Ryan.

"Yeah," I nodded, "it'll all be alright."

CHAPTER 18

In The End

My brother and I ended up moving with the boss, and it's been really fun; he's been just like a father to us. He's been helping take care of us so much, he even paid for my brother to go to college.

Things at school a lot more peaceful now too. Zabrina and Ryan don't argue as much. Josh and I are really good friends. Joaquin even came back to apologize

Autumn Jackson

for his actions and is trying to be back friends with my brother.

This just goes to show you, that you're going to need persistency in your life because it's is not going to always be easy. But you can't give up. You have to be willing to go through and just know that everything is going to be alright.

Other Books by Autumn Jackson

Too Much Drama 8-book series:

Which Should I Choose?

What Should I Do?

All Alone, All Together

Where Will Life Take Me?

Will I Make A Change?

The Unexpected Turn

The Forgotten Truth

The Last Step of the Way

(*Books 2-8 to be released May-Nov 2020)

Interested in having Autumn speak at *your* next event?

Visit: www.WeAreAPS.com and complete the contact form.

Or, send an email to:

apsnternational@gmail.com

Topics include:

The Importance of Persistence

Making Good Choices

Overcoming Peer Pressure

www.ingramcontent.com/pod-product-compliance
Lightning Source LLC
Chambersburg PA
CBHW060752180626
46818CB00002B/544